To Ellie

Merry Christmas!

Love,

Auntie Andrea

Redheaded Robbie's Christmas Story

Story by Bill Luttrell and Illustrations by Luc Melanson

Sleeping Bear Press

To Carol, Laura, and Lisa, the loves of my life.

—B.L.

To my sons, Julien and Frédéric.

—L.M.

Sleeping Bear Press

Text copyright © 2002 Bill Luttrell
Illustrations copyright © 2003 Luc Melanson

Sleeping Bear Press
310 North Main Street
Chelsea, MI 48118
www.sleepingbearpress.com

Sleeping Bear Press is an imprint of The Gale Group, Inc.,
a division of Thomson Learning, Inc.

Printed and bound in Canada.

10 9 8 7 6 5 4 3 2 1

Library of Congress Cataloging-in-Publication Data on File
ISBN: 1-58536-136-4

Early Monday morning Mrs. Wallace
stood in front of her second-grade class and
reached into the hat that was sitting on her desk.
She pulled out a piece of paper and held it high.

She said, "In my hand is the name of a lucky second-grader.
This child will get to make up a Christmas story
and tell it to the Christmas assembly this Friday."

"Choose me," bellowed Big Eddie,
the boy whose dad owned the toy store.

"Choose me," commented Cool Katie,
the coolest girl in class.

"Choose me," mumbled Munching Max,
the skinny kid who was always eating.

"Bogle bree chee,"
replied Redheaded Robbie.

Mrs. Wallace frowned.
Robbie could feel his face turning red,
and he dropped his head to his desk.
He had done it again. Robbie meant to say,
"Don't choose me," but instead,
"Bogle bree chee," came out.

Redheaded Robbie spoke perfectly fine
when talking to his parents or his friends.
But whenever Robbie felt nervous, or excited, or upset,
the first words that jumped from his lips usually made
no sense. Robbie's garbled words were funny,
but his classmates never laughed. They liked Robbie.
He shared his lunch treats. He didn't hog the swing.
In fact, when Robbie misspoke,
the kids usually covered up for him.

Big Eddie said, "Redheaded Robbie didn't
mean that, Mrs. Wallace. He's just nervous."

Mrs. Wallace read from the slip of paper. "The winner is Robbie."

"Oh no," said Big Eddie.

"It can't be so," said Cool Katie.

"Bad show," said Munching Max.

"Pupper frow,"
said Redheaded Robbie.

That night Robbie felt sick to his stomach.
How could he make up a story and tell it to the
Christmas assembly without saying something silly?

Robbie wrote a tale about a snowflake that
landed on a fruitcake and thought it was a raisin.
The story was lame, and Robbie knew it.

The next day after school, Robbie visited Big Eddie at his father's toy store. Robbie found him spinning around in his father's desk chair.

"How's the story going, Redheaded Robbie?"

"I need help," said Robbie.

Eddie said, "Make up a story about a boy who gets so many presents it takes him two days to open them all."

Robbie said, "But Christmas isn't just about getting presents. It's a time we give gifts to people who have less than us."

Eddie stopped spinning in the chair. "I never thought about Christmas that way," he said. "Sorry I didn't help with your story."

The next day after school, Robbie visited Cool Katie at her house.
He found her at her desk, talking on the phone.

"How's the story going, Redheaded Robbie?"

"I need help," said Robbie.

Katie said, "Make up a story about a cool girl
who throws a cool Christmas party."

Robbie said, "But Christmas isn't a time for being cool.
It's a time for being nice to someone new, maybe someone who is shy."

Katie put down the phone. "I never thought about
Christmas that way. Sorry I didn't help."

The next day after school, Robbie visited Munching Max.
He found Max in his bedroom, staring at a box of broken candy canes.

"How's the story going, Redheaded Robbie?"

"I need help," said Robbie.

Max said, "Make up a story about a kid who is mad at his little sister
for breaking his candy canes. He hides her Christmas presents as paybacks."

Robbie said, "But Christmas isn't a time for paybacks. It's a time to forgive."

Max put down the broken candy canes. "I never thought about
Christmas that way. Sorry I didn't help."

The next morning the students and parents
gathered in the auditorium for the Christmas assembly.

The fifth grade performed a Christmas play they had written.
Only a few times did their wigs fall off their heads.

A fourth-grader played a Christmas song he had composed on the guitar.
Only a few times did he drop his guitar.

A third-grader danced a Christmas dance she had choreographed.
Only a few times did she tumble to the floor.

When the time came for the second-grade performance,
Mrs. Wallace said, "Robbie will now tell us his Christmas story."

Robbie stood before the assembly. In his hand was the story
he had written about the snowflake that thought it was a raisin.
His stomach felt like it was filled with hot candle wax.

Robbie took a deep breath and started to tell his tale.

"Wubby waisin," he said.
Robbie's face flushed burning red.
A couple of first-graders giggled.

Robbie tried again to talk.
"Gleapin gloppin glope," he said.
A couple of fifth-graders whispered to each other.

Again Robbie tried to speak.
"Shamina mina flanket," he said.
A couple of fourth-graders pointed at Robbie.

His story was a disaster.
Robbie felt ready to burst into
tears, and he put his hands over his eyes.

Suddenly, Big Eddie left his seat and walked to the stage.
He stood next to Robbie and put his arm around him.

"Redheaded Robbie knows a Christmas story.
It's about a boy who thought that Christmas meant one thing:
getting presents. Then a little angel with red hair visited that boy.
The angel told him that Christmas is a time for giving to people
who don't have much. After the angel left, the boy asked his parents
to give some of his presents to the kids at the homeless shelter.
That's Redheaded Robbie's Christmas story."

Cool Katie left her seat.

She stood next to Robbie and held his hand.

"Redheaded Robbie knows a Christmas story of a girl
who thought that Christmas was all about being cool.
Then a little angel with red hair visited that girl.
The angel told her that Christmas is a time for
being nice to someone new, maybe someone who is shy.
After the angel left, that girl visited a shy girl and played with her.
That's Redheaded Robbie's Christmas story."

Munching Max got up from his seat.

He stood next to Robbie and slid a bag of peanuts into Robbie's pocket.

"Redheaded Robbie knows a Christmas story.
It's about a kid who wanted to hide his little sister's
Christmas presents as paybacks for breaking his candy canes.
Then a little angel with red hair visited the kid.
The angel told him that Christmas is a time to forgive, not to pay back.
After the angel left, that kid forgave his little sister and took her sledding.
That's Redheaded Robbie's Christmas story."

The assembly stood and clapped.

They didn't stop until Mrs. Wallace stood next to Robbie and asked for quiet.

She wiped away a tear and said,

"Thank you, Robbie, for your wonderful Christmas stories!

Let each person here follow Robbie's advice.

Give before you take.

Show kindness to someone new.

Forgive a person who has hurt you."

Mrs. Wallace looked at Robbie. "Did I forget to say anything?"

"Hurry Hickmas to all!"

said Redheaded Robbie.

The End